The Barbie™ as

The Princess

and the Pauper

Barbie™ as The Princess and the Pauper

A Junior Novelization

Adapted by Linda Williams Aber
from the original screenplay by
Cliff Ruby and Elana Lesser

SCHOLASTIC INC.

New York   Toronto   London   Auckland   Sydney
Mexico City   New Delhi   Hong Kong   Buenos Aires

ISBN 0-439-63600-0
Designed by Louise Bova

BARBIE and associated trademarks and trade dress are
owned by and used under license from Mattel, Inc.
Copyright © 2004 Mattel Inc. All Rights Reserved.

Published by Scholastic Inc.
SCHOLASTIC and associated logos are trademarks and/or
registered trademarks of Scholastic Inc.

Special thanks to Rob Hudnut, Shelley Tabbut, Vicki Jaeger, Monica Lopez, Jesyca C. Durchin, and Mainframe Entertainment

Photography by Tom Wolfson, Willy Lew, Shirley Ushirogata, Laura Lynch, Lin Carlson, Lars Auvinen, Johannes Auvinen, Rebecca Stillman, Keith Biele, Karl Polverino, David Chickering, Susan Cracraft, Vicki Tran, Lisa Bellow, Chang-Chin Wang, Brian Johnson, Heidi Waldorf, Susanne Briant, Scott Meskill, Steve Toth, Judy Tsuno, and Lisa Collins

Music: "Free," "I Am a Girl Like You," and "If You Love Me for Me": Lyrics by Amy Powers. All other songs: Lyrics by Amy Powers and Rob Hudnut.

10   9   8   7   6   5   4   3   2   1   04   05   06   07   08

Printed in the U.S.A.
First printing, October 2004

Introduction

Long ago and far away, in a village high on a mountaintop, something amazing happened. Two identical baby girls were born at the very same time. One was a princess named Anneliese. The other was a girl named Erika, born to poor parents in the village.

The two girls looked exactly alike. But they led very different lives. Princess Anneliese lived in a beautiful castle. She learned how to behave like a Princess. She studied with a handsome young tutor named Julian.

Erika lived in a one-room apartment. She worked long hours sewing dresses. The cruel owner of the dressmaking shop, Madame Carp, wanted to keep Erika working for her for a long, long time.

With lives so different, it wasn't surprising that the two girls had never met. But one day, destiny made their paths cross. From that day forward, the lives of the Princess and the Pauper were changed forever. . . .

Chapter 1
A Royal Problem

Princess Anneliese was having a perfect day. The sun shone on her blond hair. She and her cat, Serafina, were in the royal gardens. The Princess was doing her royal science homework. She studied a tiny bee sitting on a big red rose. Suddenly, the bee left the rose and flew to the cat's nose!

"Don't worry, Serafina," the Princess said sweetly. "It's just a little honeybee."

Princess Anneliese laughed at the funny face her cat made. The bee flew away, but they were not alone for long. "There you are, your highness," a voice said.

It was the Royal Scheduler. He was in charge of making sure the Princess was on time for all of her royal duties. "We're late, late, late!" he cried. "First you have your royal fitting for your

wedding dress. Then you have to make a speech."

Princess Anneliese and Serafina followed the Royal Scheduler inside the castle. They went to the royal chambers where the Royal Maid was waiting with a very beautiful wedding dress for the Princess. Her carefree outdoor time was over. Instead of thinking about flowers and bees,

Princess Anneliese had to think about a wedding she didn't want. It was her own marriage to a rich young king who was seeking a wife. He was King Dominick, a man she'd never even met.

Secretly, the Princess was in love with her Royal Tutor, Julian. But a Princess could not marry a teacher. She had to marry a member of a royal family.

"All my life, I've always wanted to have one day just for me," the Princess told her cat. "I just want one day to be free! Free to listen to my heart and marry whom I choose."

Anneliese looked up as her mother, Queen Genevieve, came into the room. "I'm so sorry, my darling," her mother said. "But you know you must marry King Dominick. My Royal Advisor, Preminger, has informed me our royal gold mines are empty. There won't be enough money to take care of the people of our kingdom. I've arranged for you to marry King Dominick so our two kingdoms will be joined together. Then we will be able to care for our people. It's your royal duty."

"I know," Anneliese said sadly. "But it's also my royal problem."

Chapter 2
A Bad Idea

"How dare the Queen make a decision without me!" Preminger shouted as he arrived at the royal gold mine. He had just heard the plans for Princess Anneliese's marriage.

In the darkness of the mine, Preminger's helpers, Nick and Nack, shook as their master spoke.

"Master Preminger!" Nick said nervously. "You're back early. We just stole the last of the gold from the royal mine."

"Yeah," Nack added. "It's all yours."

"Yes it is," the evil Preminger said. He scooped up a handful of golden nuggets. "And my plan was that I would marry the Princess and rule the land."

"Right," said Nack, "except for this one little problem. She's marrying the King of Dulcinia next week."

"Silence!" shouted Preminger. "I have a new plan. Suppose the Princess

goes missing? Then King Dominick will say good-bye. I'll find her, bring her back, and be a hero. The Queen will be so grateful, she'll want the Princess to marry me!"

"Cool," said Nick.

"Yes." Preminger laughed. "The kingdom and the castle will be mine!"

Later, back at the castle, Princess Anneliese was busy looking through a magnifying glass at a shiny rock. She was studying her school lessons.

There was a knock at the door. "Come in," the Princess said. Her face lit up when she saw the Royal Tutor. "Julian!" she said. "What do you think? I classified this as iron pyrite, otherwise known as fool's gold."

"Good work, your highness," Julian replied, smiling. He was handsome and smart. He was also secretly in love with the Princess.

"Your highness?" Anneliese asked. "Why so formal? It's just me."

"The Queen sent me," Julian said. "The Foreign Ambassador has arrived with a gift for you. I must take you to meet him."

"He's here already?" Anneliese said sadly. But she knew her royal duty. So she followed Julian to the royal throne room.

When they arrived, the Queen, Pre-minger, the Foreign Ambassador, and his very handsome young Royal Page were waiting.

"Princess Anneliese, your highness," Julian announced.

"Come, darling," the Queen said. "Ambassador Bismark has brought you a lovely engagement gift from King Dominick. Open it!"

"Thank you," Anneliese said politely. She took the box from the handsome Royal Page and opened it. Inside was a beautiful diamond necklace. "Oh! It's stunning!" she cried.

Ambassador Bismark turned to the Queen. "May I ask if you have set a date for the wedding?" he said.

"Will a week from today do?" the Queen replied.

"Next week?" Anneliese, Julian, and Preminger all gasped.

Preminger caught himself. "A most wise and thoughtful decision, your majesty," he said to the Queen.

The Foreign Ambassador was the only one who was really pleased. "Excellent!" he said. "We will send for King Dominick so he can meet his new bride!"

Chapter 3
Seeing Double

Anneliese had many things to learn before meeting King Dominick. Julian spent the next few days teaching her all about the King's kingdom. "So, to review," he said, "King Dominick's kingdom includes . . . ?"

"Four lakes, two mountain ranges, and many apple orchards," Anneliese answered.

"Excellent!" Julian said.

Her answers were correct, but the Princess didn't feel like smiling. "What do you think this King Dominick will be like?" she asked Julian.

"I've heard he loves music," Julian replied. "He plays three different instruments. I'm sure he'll be suitable."

"I know it's the right thing to marry him," the Princess said. "But sometimes I wish I could just be free." Sadly, she looked out the window.

Julian had an idea. "Anneliese, you're going to need your cape," he said. "My grandmother always said any problem can be solved with some fresh air. We're going to the village for our lesson today!"

The Princess threw on her cape and pulled up the hood. Julian helped her into the royal carriage. Her cat,

Serafina, jumped in with her. Together the three of them rode to town.

"It feels so good to be outside the castle walls," Anneliese said as they walked through the market. "Nobody knows who I am."

When they came to a flower stall, Julian picked up a beautiful rose for Anneliese.

"My favorite," the Princess said, smelling the flower. "But you knew that."

Julian kept track of the time. Soon he left Anneliese to get the carriage. While he was gone, Anneliese heard someone singing.

"Let's go listen, Serafina," she said. They walked a little way and came to the dark-haired young girl who was singing. A scruffy alley cat sat nearby. A money cup with a few coins in it was at her feet.

Before Anneliese could place a coin in the cup, a mean-looking woman stepped into their path. She began shouting at the girl. "Here again, Erika?"

"Madame Carp!" the girl exclaimed.

Madame Carp grabbed the money cup and took the coins.

"I earned that money," the girl cried.

"And you owe it to me," Madame Carp snapped. "Do you really think you can make a living as a singer? Get back to work in my dressmaking shop at once!"

The awful woman threw the empty cup over her shoulder. Then she left.

The girl named Erika bent down to pick it up. To her surprise, a large gold coin fell into the cup. "Thank you," she said as she looked up. She was eye to eye with Anneliese.

Anneliese was amazed. "You look just like me!" she said to the girl.

"I was going to say you look just like me," the girl replied.

"What's your name?" Anneliese asked.

"Erika," the girl answered. "And this is my cat, Wolfie. And you are . . . ?

"Please call me Anneliese," the Princess said. "And this is my cat, Serafina." The two cats smiled at each other. They liked each other instantly.

"You have the same name as the Princess," Erika said to Anneliese. But then she realized that Anneliese really was the Princess! Erika bowed to her. "Aren't you supposed to be inside the castle?"

Anneliese sighed. "This is my last taste of freedom. I'm getting married next week to a total stranger."

"At least you're not a servant to Madame Carp," Erika replied. "I dream of freedom, too."

"I can't believe it," Anneliese said. "Except for our hair, we could be twins. But what about this?" The Princess pulled aside the shoulder of her dress. She showed Erika a crown-shaped birthmark on her shoulder.

"No," Erika said, showing the Princess her shoulder. "I don't have that birthmark. But everything else is the same."

Just then, Julian returned. When he saw Erika and Anneliese together, he was surprised. "You look like twins!" he cried.

The three new friends talked for a while longer. Finally, Julian had to end the visit. "I'm sorry, your highness," he said to Anneliese. "We should be getting back."

Anneliese turned to her new friend. "One day you must sing for us at the castle," she said.

"Me?" Erika replied. "I'd be honored, your highness."

"I'll send someone for you," the Princess promised. "Where do you live?"

"At Madame Carp's, the dressmaker's house," Erika said.

Anneliese stepped into the carriage that was waiting. "Bye, Erika," she said sweetly. "I won't forget."

Chapter 4
The Missing Princess

Anneliese slept soundly that night. She was dreaming of her lovely day out. But suddenly, a loud yowl from Serafina woke her. The princess sat up in her bed and looked around her room. Serafina's bed was empty.

"Serafina?" Anneliese said. "Where are you?"

Another yowl drew her out to the gardens to look for her cat. "Come here, girl," she said. "Come here, kitty."

Suddenly, a dark sack covered Anneliese's head. She was lifted into a horse-drawn cart, which sped away.

"I order you to turn this cart around right now!" the Princess shouted. But she couldn't see anything.

Finally, the cart ride ended and Anneliese was locked inside a strange room inside a stone house.

"I command you to unlock the door," she cried. No one answered her cries.

"Is she here?" Preminger asked.

"Signed, sealed, and delivered," his helper Nack replied.

"Does she know I'm behind this?" Preminger asked.

"Not a clue, master," said his other helper, Nick.

"Keep her here until the wedding to King Dominick is canceled," Preminger ordered. "Then we'll see who the Princess marries!"

Back at the castle, morning arrived as usual. The Queen knocked on the door of the Princess's room. "Anneliese? Are you here?"

Preminger stepped in front of the Queen. He bowed and then opened the door for her. The room was empty.

"Where could she be?" the Queen asked. "She wasn't at breakfast."

"Is that something on her desk, your majesty?" Preminger said.

The Queen walked over to Anneliese's writing desk. There was a letter addressed to her, so she opened it — and gasped. "It says she's run away so she won't have to marry King Dominick," the Queen cried.

Preminger tried not to smile. "Oh!" he said. "That is awful!"

"We have to find her," the Queen declared. "She could be hurt. Oh, my poor darling."

"I'll send out search parties at once," Preminger said. "I'm sure she hasn't gotten far."

"Oh, Preminger," sighed the Queen, "what would I do without you?"

Later that day, the Queen met with Ambassador Bismark. Julian and Preminger were there, too.

"This is an outrage!" Ambassador Bismark cried. "I insist we cancel the wedding if the Princess doesn't return by the end of the day."

"It doesn't make sense," Julian said. "I can't see Anneliese just running away."

"See for yourself," Preminger said. He handed Julian the letter.

Julian smelled the letter. Then he turned to Preminger. "I'll help you look for her," he said.

"I think I can handle that on my own," Preminger snapped at Julian. "Why don't you stick to your books, tutor?"

Preminger snatched the letter from

Julian and left. But something was bothering Julian. *She never scented her paper with lilac,* he thought. *It was always rose.*

Julian didn't trust Preminger. But he had a plan that he hoped would help bring back the Princess.

Chapter 5
Julian's Plan

Julian dashed out of the castle in a horse-drawn carriage. He rode through the village. Finally, he stopped the carriage in front of Madame Carp's door.

"Welcome, sir," Madame Carp said when she saw the handsome, well-dressed man. "Are you looking for a gown for a special lady?"

"If I may," Julian said politely, "I would like to speak to one of your dressmakers — Miss Erika."

Madame Carp's mouth dropped open.

Erika stepped forward. "I don't believe it," she said. "The Princess sent for me! I'm going to sing at the castle. Me!"

Julian escorted Erika and her cat, Wolfie, to the carriage. "I'm sorry, Erika," he said. "I haven't come to bring you to the castle to sing. You see, the Princess is missing. I need you to help me find her."

"Me? What can I do?" Erika asked.

"Pretend to be Princess Anneliese," Julian replied.

"Me?" Erika said again.

"Just listen," Julian said. "I believe Preminger, our Royal Advisor, has taken the Princess away. He wants the royal wedding to be called off."

"That's terrible," Erika gasped.

"You look just like her," Julian explained. "If you pretend to be the Princess for a short time, the wedding won't be called off. Then I can trick Preminger into showing where he's hiding her."

"That's quite a plan," Erika said. "There's just one little teeny problem. No one in the world would believe I'm a Princess!"

Julian smiled. "Leave that to me," he said.

Julian drove the carriage back through the castle gates. He secretly slipped Erika and Wolfie inside Anneliese's bedroom. "You'll be safe in here, Erika," he said.

Erika almost didn't hear Julian. She

was busy looking around the room. "Look at the size of this place!" she exclaimed.

Then Erika and Julian saw her reflection in the mirror. "The likeness is amazing," he said.

"Except for my hair," said Erika.

"I've thought of everything," Julian replied. He pulled out a blond wig and

placed it on her head. And for the next few hours, he gave Erika lessons on how to be a perfect Princess.

As the clock struck seven, Erika was ready to be presented to the Queen and her guests. With fingers crossed for luck, she followed Julian to the throne room.

Julian peeked through the door. Ambassador Bismark and his Royal Page were standing before the Queen. Preminger stood by her side.

"It's official, then," the Foreign Ambassador said. "Due to the disappearance of the Princess, the wedding to King Dominick is called off."

Preminger smiled. He thought his plan was working.

Suddenly, Julian burst into the room. "Your highness, wait!" he said. "May I present — Princess Anneliese."

Everyone turned to look as "Princess" Erika walked into the room. She curtsied to the Queen.

"Darling!" the Queen cried happily. "You're back! Where have you been?"

Preminger's eyes opened wide. He was waiting for the Princess to tell the Queen all about the kidnapping. But to his surprise, she had a different story.

"I'm sorry," she said. "I shouldn't have run away."

"Promise me you'll never do it again," the Queen said.

"I promise," Erika replied.

"The wedding is back on," Ambassador Bismark announced. "King Dominick is due tomorrow."

"Wonderful!" said the Queen. "And then only three short days before the wedding."

Preminger looked very nervous. "I must be off to see to the . . . er . . . arrangements," he said, leaving quickly. Julian was right behind him.

As Preminger walked to the door, he tripped over Erika's cat, Wolfie. "Who let this mangy beast in here?" Preminger roared.

"You seem nervous," Julian said. "Is everything all right?"

Preminger glared at Julian. "It soon will be," he snarled as he stomped off.

Wolfie sniffed at a pine needle left by Preminger's boot. Julian picked up the needle. "Hmm," he said, "a needle from a silver fir tree. What's Preminger doing in the western forest?"

But before Julian could leave, the Queen stopped him. "Julian, wait. I want to hear all about how you found Anneliese."

Julian had no choice but to stay. "Of course, your majesty," he said.

Chapter 6
Anneliese,
the Village Princess

Meanwhile, the real Princess was still being held captive. But she had a plan. She disguised Serafina as a ghost, then shrieked for help. When her kidnappers came into the room, they were terrified. Anneliese locked Nick and Nack in the room, and she and Serafina escaped! They climbed into the horse-drawn cart that was tied up outside. The Princess drove the cart toward the castle.

When Nick and Nack realized that they had been tricked by the Princess, they were terrified. What would they tell their master? He was due to arrive any second.

They were right. Seconds later, Preminger pounded on the door. "Let me in, you idiots!" he shouted.

"How did she escape?" Preminger growled.

"Who?" Nack asked. He was surprised that his master knew the Princess was gone.

Preminger marched inside and threw open the door to the room where the Princess should have been. But instead of Anneliese, he found only Nick.

Meanwhile, thanks to the pine needle clue, Julian had no trouble tracking

Preminger to the western forest. He got off his horse and silently crept up to the window of the chalet. He peeked in just in time to see Preminger holding Nick and Nack by the collar.

"I can figure out how the Princess escaped from you fools," Preminger shouted. "But why didn't she tell the Queen she'd been captured? Something's odd. I must solve this Princess puzzle if I am to be King. Stay here!"

Julian couldn't believe his ears. "King? Preminger?"

A twig cracked under Julian's foot, and he froze. But it was too late. The door burst open and Preminger rushed outside.

Julian spoke first. "Preminger? How can you be King?" he asked. He didn't notice Nick and Nack creeping up behind him. They captured him!

Preminger laughed. "How can I be King?" he repeated. "You're the tutor. You're supposed to have all the answers."

Anneliese and Serafina arrived at the castle. But the gates were closed and a guard stood by them. "Who goes there?" the guard called out.

"Princess Anneliese," Anneliese replied.

The guard just laughed. "That's a good one!"

"You are speaking to the Princess,"

Anneliese insisted. "Please let me through."

"Really?" the guard said. "Then how come I just saw the Princess eating dinner with the Queen? Now move along before I lose my temper. Go on now."

Anneliese had no choice. She turned the cart around and headed for

the village. She came to a tavern. Light spilled onto the cobblestone street and music played. "We'll find help in here," she said to her cat.

As the Princess walked to the door of the tavern, Madame Carp came out. "Erika! You lazy girl!" she shouted. "What did you do to your hair? Well, it

doesn't matter. You're coming with me!" In no time, Madame Carp put Anneliese to work in her dressmaker's shop.

"I am Princess Anneliese," the Princess insisted.

"You don't look a thing like the Princess," Madame Carp said. "Now be quiet and get back to work."

"If you're going to treat your workers this way, I'm going to report you to the Queen," Anneliese said. "I'm warning you."

"You're warning me?" Madame Carp laughed. "We'll see about that. You're not coming out until every dress is finished, Erika."

The door slammed shut and the key turned in the lock. Anneliese was locked in again.

Anneliese had an idea. She couldn't get

out, but perhaps Serafina could! She snipped a label from a dress. MADE EXCLUSIVELY BY MADAME CARP, the label read. She took off her royal ring and tied it to Serafina's collar with the label.

"Okay, Serafina," Anneliese said. "It's up to you now. Take this to the castle. When somebody sees the label, it will lead them here."

Serafina climbed through the window and disappeared into the night.

Chapter 7
The King and the Pauper

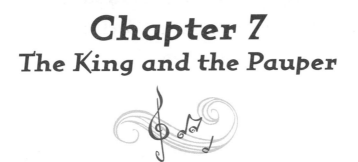

Erika liked Anneliese's life much more than Anneliese liked Erika's life. Sunlight poured through the castle window and into the bedroom where Erika slept. "I thought I was dreaming," she said. "But thank goodness I'm not."

There was a knock at the door. A maid came in carrying a breakfast tray. "Your breakfast, your highness," said the maid.

"Really?" Erika said. "In bed?"

"As always," said the maid.

"Yes, of course," Erika replied. "Thank you." She held out a scone to the maid. "Please, take some," she said. "There's plenty."

"Thank you, my lady," said the maid. "I'll draw your bath. Would you like bubbles? Mineral salts? Lavender oil?"

"Everything!" Erika replied happily.

The maid disappeared into the bathroom.

"Like the good life, don't you?" Erika said to Wolfie. "This will only last as long as we don't give ourselves away."

In another room in the castle, Ambassador Bismark was talking to his page. He was worried. "You mean you're going to just tell her that you disguised yourself as a page?" Bismark said. "Are you sure that's wise, your majesty?"

The Royal Page took off his cap and stood tall. Without his cap, he looked more like a king than a page. In fact, this page was really King Dominick!

"No, I'm not sure," King Dominick said. "But I have to be honest. I think she'll understand. I didn't want to marry a stranger any more than she did."

"But King Dominick," the Foreign Ambassador said, "she may call off the wedding again."

"All the more reason to explain now," said the King. "I want her to understand why I dressed as a page. I want her to like me for myself, not just because I'm King."

King Dominick went toward the Princess's room. He was about to knock when he heard Erika's beautiful singing. *She sings like an angel,* he thought. Suddenly shy, he backed away and went directly to tell the Queen what he had done.

"Thank you for your understanding," King Dominick said to the Queen.

"And thank you," the Queen replied,

"for being so understanding about the delay in the wedding plans. But it's all sorted out now."

Just then, Preminger entered the throne room. Erika — dressed like the Princess — was right behind him. "May I announce — Princess Anneliese," Preminger said.

"Hello, my darling," said the Queen. "Come in. I want to introduce you to King Dominick. He has something he wants to tell you."

The King bowed to Erika. "I'm honored," he said.

"The honor is mine, King Dominick," Erika replied.

"Please call me Dominick," said the King.

"Call me Eri — I mean, Anneliese,"

Erika said. "Princess Anneliese, that's my name."

The King looked confused, but he smiled. "I'm sure you're wondering why I disguised myself as a page," he said.

"You did? I mean, yes, uh, why did you?" Erika asked.

"I wanted to meet you without all

this ceremony," the King explained. "I wanted to get to know the real you."

"King Dominick," the Queen interrupted, "would you do us the honor of playing the harpsichord? I know you love music."

Erika's eyes lit up. "You do?" she asked.

"I will play," the King agreed, "if the Princess will sing with me."

"What a great idea," the Queen said. "Sing, darling."

The couple began a duet while the Queen and Preminger looked on. The King and the Princess seemed to be a perfect couple.

Erika and the King spent the day together, walking and talking. At the end of the day, King Dominick looked into

Erika's eyes. "There's something about you," he said. "You're honest. I like that." He said good night and left the Princess.

"Did you hear that, Wolfie?" Erika said to her cat. "He thinks I'm honest. Oh, how did I get into this mess? Julian and the real Princess are still missing. And now I think I'm falling in love with the King!"

Chapter 8
All's Well That Ends Well

After a long and difficult trip up the mountain, Serafina finally made it back to the castle. But unfortunately, the first person she ran into was Preminger.

"Well, well," he said, picking her up. "Where have you been?" Serafina hissed and tried to escape. But it was no use. Preminger noticed the royal ring on Serafina's collar. "The Princess's ring," he said as he read the label. "Madame Carp's dressmaker's shop. Maybe that is the answer to our mystery."

Preminger wasted no time. He went to Madame Carp's shop and broke open the door. "Princess Anneliese! Is that really you?" he said when he saw the Princess.

"Preminger, you found my ring!" Anneliese exclaimed. "Thank goodness!"

"Come quickly, Princess. You can tell me everything on the way to the castle."

Preminger put Anneliese in the carriage, and they raced away. But they weren't going to the castle. Preminger was taking the Princess down into the gold mine! Nick and Nack were waiting for them there.

When Anneliese saw where they

were, she gasped. "What are we doing here?"

"Taking a little side trip, Princess," he replied.

"To the royal mine?" she asked. "Aha! So *you* were behind this!"

"Very clever, finding a double to fool the Queen," Preminger said. "But not quite clever enough. Checkmate. I win."

"I don't understand, Preminger," Anneliese said. "Why would you do this?"

"To be King," Preminger replied. "With all the riches of the mines in my hands, I'm the one who will be getting married."

"I would never marry you," Anneliese cried.

Preminger laughed. "Not you,

Princess. I've found a new bride. Your mother is a *very* handsome woman."

Preminger swung open a steel door and pushed Anneliese and her cat inside. To her surprise, Julian was tied up on the wet floor of the room. She rushed to him and tried to untie him.

"How sad your mother will be when

they discover you've both died in a tragic mine accident," Preminger said.

"She'll never give up looking for the Princess," Julian yelled.

"Oh, I think she will," Preminger sneered, "when I show her this!" He held up the royal ring. The ring would be proof that the Princess was dead.

With a laugh, Preminger slammed the door shut and bolted it. Before he left, his helpers blocked the entrance to the mines.

"Oh, Julian," the Princess cried. "I never wanted to marry the King. It was you I was in love with, the man who has taught me so much."

Julian smiled sadly. "I've dreamed I'd hear those words from you. But I'm not a king. I can't give you what he can."

"I think you're like this rock," Anneliese said, holding up a stone. She pulled the pieces apart, and inside were brilliant purple crystals. "You're unassuming on the outside, but a treasure within."

Back at the castle, the Queen had no idea that her real daughter was in such trouble. She thought everything was in order. She signed a scroll in front of Ambassador Bismark, King Dominick, and Erika. "The kingdoms will be officially joined after the wedding tomorrow," she said to Erika. "Are you ready?"

Before Erika could answer, the door flew open. Preminger and his helpers came in. Preminger pointed at Erika. "Grab her!" he ordered. "She is not the real Princess!"

Nick and Nack grabbed Erika. "Let go," the girl cried.

"She's a fake," Preminger continued. "A common pauper, not the Princess at all."

"Are you telling me I don't know my own daughter?" asked the Queen.

"I just found out the truth," Preminger lied. "Julian hid the Princess so this fake princess could take her place, marry King Dominick, and take over the kingdom."

"And what proof do you have of this silly story?" King Dominick asked.

Preminger handed the Queen the royal ring. "This is all my workers found in the rubble at the gold mine." He pointed a finger at Erika. "Check her shoulder. There's no royal birthmark, I assure you."

The Queen looked at Erika's shoulder. "It's true," she said sadly.

"I don't believe it," said King Dominick. He turned to Erika, waiting for her to explain.

"I'm s-sorry," Erika stammered. "I can explain. I just wanted to save the Princess from him!" she said, pointing to Preminger. "We have to find Julian."

"Yes," said Preminger. "Julian planned everything. Throw this fake princess into the dungeon!"

Nick and Nack led Erika to the

dungeon. They left behind a very angry Foreign Ambassador. "Do you take us for fools?" he said. "You tried to marry King Dominick off to a pauper. The sooner we leave the better!"

The Foreign Ambassador and the King left. Ambassador Bismark slammed the door behind them.

Preminger was happy. His plan was working. He was going to ask the Queen to marry him. He would offer the Queen his fortune in return for her hand. But of course he really planned to keep it all for himself.

Erika's days as the Princess were over. She was in the dungeon, asleep on a cot. She only had Wolfie for company.

A noise outside the dungeon got Wolfie's attention. It was the horse from Preminger's carriage!

Wolfie slipped through the bars and followed the horse.

A little while later, the horse stopped in front of the collapsed gold mine entrance. Wolfie sniffed around until he found an old mine shaft. He bravely jumped down the shaft, falling into the dim tunnel.

Instead of landing on the bottom of the shaft, though, he crashed into a small storeroom.

Julian and Anneliese were very

surprised when Wolfie burst through the storeroom ceiling.

"It's Erika's cat!" Anneliese cried.

"It's an old mine shaft," Julian said, as he peered up the tunnel.

Anneliese glanced down at the puddles of water on the floor. A trickle was oozing out from underneath a large boulder. She had an idea. "Help me," Anneliese said to Julian.

Together they pushed the boulder

until it rolled away. Water began to bubble up from the hole where the boulder had been.

Anneliese grabbed the cats and climbed into a barrel. Julian jumped in, too, as the water level rose in the storeroom.

Quickly, the water carried the barrel up the mine shaft toward freedom.

Chapter 9
A Royal Wedding

Back at the castle, Erika was still trapped in the dungeon. Until . . . a guard appeared. "Her highness wants to see you," he said, leading Erika out of her cell.

Erika followed him. And then she saw her chance. She stepped on his foot as hard as she could — then ran.

"Wait!" said the guard. He grabbed her arm. Then he lifted the visor on his helmet. It was King Dominick!

"Dominick!" Erika gasped. "I can explain. . . ."

"No need," said the King. "I don't believe you're the person Preminger says you are."

In the castle's garden, Preminger was walking down the aisle wearing royal robes. The Queen joined him. "Smile, my dear," Preminger said to her. "You're about to be my queen."

"Only to save my people," the Queen replied. "Your fortune will help them all."

Suddenly, a voice in the crowd shouted, "Wait! Wait! Stop the wedding!"

"Anneliese?" the Queen cried. "Is it you?"

"This is the fake princess," Preminger shouted. "She must have escaped from the dungeon."

"No, Preminger," Anneliese said. She lowered her sleeve and showed her royal birthmark.

"It is you, my darling," the Queen said happily. She hugged her daughter.

Preminger knew he was in big trouble. He started to run, but he didn't get far. Outside the castle walls, King Dominick was waiting. He blocked Preminger's path.

Nick and Nack were in trouble, too. They tried to escape. But Erika and Anneliese were there to stop them! Before they knew what was happening, Preminger and his two henchmen were locked in the castle dungeon — for good.

That evening, the Queen had a lot to say. "Preminger played me for a fool.

When I think what might have happened . . ."

"But it didn't happen," Anneliese said. "Thanks to the man I love, Julian. Mother, it's Julian I want to marry."

"I want you to be happy, but our kingdom is in trouble," the Queen said.

"I think I can change that," Anneliese said. "When Julian and I were trapped in the mines, we discovered crystals. They are worth more than gold. Our kingdom is rich again!"

New plans for a wedding were made. But this time the wedding was for *two* royal couples. Princess Anneliese married her Royal Tutor, and Erika married King Dominick. And so

both the Princess and the Pauper lived
happily ever after. . . .